I0600994

Not Entirely

Human

AND OTHER STORIES

HEATHER EWINGS

Quamby Press

Contents

Thank you for reading! Within these pages you'll find an odd collection of speculative microfiction—historical, supernatural, fantasy, sci-fi – the longest no more than 342 words.

More of my short stories can be found at medium.com/@heatherewings, or you can find out more about me and my books at www.heatherewings.com.au

Not Entirely Human

There was a pregnancy, so there had to be a boyfriend.

I certainly couldn't tell them there'd been no one for months... Just one lonely night in the forest, comforted by a creature not entirely human.

I told them I was going to bring him round for dinner... I told them we'd been seeing each other for a while now, that he was special... Maybe even The One.

When the day of the dinner came I rang up in hysterics, there'd been an accident, he hadn't made it. I locked myself away, refused to see anyone, gratefully accepted the casseroles left on my doorstep.

It wasn't until I was showing I made contact, revealed the pregnancy, claimed I'd been too lost in grief to register the missed periods, the sore breasts, the vomiting that must've been morning sickness, not heart break.

If the babe had looked normal I might've got away with it, but that faintly green skin, those too-big eyes... every one knows they're the mark of the fae folk.

Everyone knows I lied.

One Wish

The newborn was placed on her mother's stomach, sticky and pink as a watermelon.

Her fairy godmother hovered above. 'What do you wish for her?'

'A life free from anxiety.'

The magic wand was waved, and the fairy smiled. 'Done.'

Shadows

The sun set, casting long shadows Ella liked to play in. The creatures of the dusk joined her; creeping, creeping, leaping, creeping. But night came quickly, and the dusk creatures feared the night. They said farewell and Ella returned to her parent's hearth, safe from the silent stalkers who feared the dancing flames. Life had always been this way; her parents never ventured into the dark, nor theirs before them. Now Ella patrolled the fire's edge, her bow notched and ready. Her children would need no fire for safety, her dusky friends would have nought to fear.

Rescue

The man jams a stick in the creature's side.

Blood wells, but he cups his hand under its chin, catching tears that solidify as they fall, forming perfect crystals.

He holds them out to Rin. "Two thousand yen."

Rin shakes her head. "I didn't know."

He grunts. "The samebito? It's a monster. Doesn't feel anything."

All day, Rin watches.

When the man has a break she unlatches the cage.

"You're free."

The samebito's eyes water, crystals spilling, bouncing on the ground to ping against the metal bars.

"Thank you." She whispers, taking Rin's hands to cry into them.

"Thank you."

Who Caught Who?

A crow landed on the railing.

"Watch." Aito nudged Eiji, and held out some meat.

"It won't come that close," Eiji said.

It did, snatching the meat and swallowing it whole.

"Bet you can't get it inside."

Aito eased the door behind him open and crept backwards, holding out another piece of meat.

The crow's head tilted to one side.

"Come on," Aito murmured.

It hopped through the door, and Eiji pulled it shut.

"Got him."

Laughter echoed. Suddenly there wasn't a crow with them, but a man.

"Karasu-tengu!" Eiji gasped.

"Yes. And I think you'll find, I've got you."

Christmas Wedding

Elizabeth ran her hands over her grey woollen skirt. Butterflies danced in her stomach and she dismissed them; foolish, at her stage of life. John was a good man. There weren't many who would take on a widow with five children. And he helped with young Henry when others averted their eyes, unwilling to take in the boy's enlarged head, laboured breathing, or the fact he could not sit properly despite being three years of age.

She glanced at the small gathering. Pastor Lelean had been kind to give up his home on Christmas Day, of all days. He held Robert in his arms, the lad squirming to get down and run around with the other children now he'd finally found his feet. Mrs Downey held Henry, and Elizabeth's heart warmed to see her son was managing to hold his head up today. Lizzie, Sarah and Thomas were running around with the Downey children.

"Are we ready?" The Pastor asked.

Elizabeth nodded, and the group moved inside to the parlour, where the Pastor conducted the ceremony.

It went by in a blur, first John and then Elizabeth repeating their vows of honour and commitment.

When it was done Mrs Downey wrapped Elizabeth in a congratulatory hug. Miss Westwood shook John's hand. Only Thomas stood back, a frown on his face.

Elizabeth reached out an arm to him, and he raced over, burying his head in her shoulder.

"I know you miss your da," she said. "And John won't ever replace him, but he's a good man. He'll look after us, and we need that now."

Weaving Fate

'Hmm...' Grandmother Fate peered across her shimmering web. 'This story... and that story...' She stretched out her long limbs, pulling the sticky strands together, weaving them in and out, close here, further apart there, tighter and tighter until they became a single thread.

On earth they bumped into each other, his daughter's icecream leaving a sticky smear on her dress.

'I'm so sorry.' He offered her napkins to wipe herself down.

'It's fine.' She accepted them, cleaning away the worst of it. 'Not like it hasn't happened before.' She nodded to her sleeping toddler in the pram, and glanced up to meet his gaze.

Their eyes sparked, faces flushing as each turned away.

'My husband — ' she began.

'My wife — ' he explained.

They bustled away, too scared to look back.

In the heavens Grandmother Fate smiled. 'One day,' she promised them. 'One day.'

Arthur Gordon

Charles returned to the house, Dr Armitage hot on his heels. May sat by the window, staring vacantly out onto the road, leaving little Arthur listless in his cot. The two older children were nowhere to be seen.

"I sent 'em off to play," May said. "They don't need to see another death."

Charles frowned. "We don't know that — "

"Your wife is correct, Mr Tilley." The doctor interrupted. "Arthur is suffering from Marasmus."

Charles glared at him, still standing in the doorway. "Speak plainly!"

"Malnutrition."

"You can't tell from there. Attend to the boy."

Dr Armitage refused to budge. "I've told you before. Look at him. Your son is near six months old, yet he is little larger than a newborn." He shook his head. "I'm very sorry Mr Tilley, there is nothing I can do." He nodded to May. "My condolences, Mrs Tilley."

She watched him leave.

"I told you we never should've come 'ere." May turned to Charles. "Three children in five years, and not one of 'em made it to their first birthday. Should've stayed where we were. This place is cursed."

Charles shook his head and moved to sit with Arthur. The boy just needed some sustenance, that was all. If May's milk hadn't dried up so early... He shook his head. There was nothing to be done about that. He'd hoped desperately this child would survive. That Arthur would be the one to bring joy back to May's eyes. He picked up the lad, barely strong enough to move his eyes to look at his father. The boy blinked, his eyelids heavy, then sighed. His head lolled backwards.

He was gone.

Tea with Grandma

The room was warm with candlelight, despite the icy wind that shook the windows and rained leaves on the roof.

In the centre of the room Frances knelt by a low table, setting a cup of tea and a plate of biscuits in front of a photo of an elderly woman. She closed her eyes and whispered a prayer.

When Frances opened her eyes the elderly woman, barely more substantial than the steam rising from the cup, was sitting in the armchair, cup in hand, dipping a biscuit in the tea.

"Grandma?"

"I wondered when you'd call me. You're older than I expected you would be."

"I found your journals."

Grandma laughed. "I wouldn't be here if you hadn't." She took a sip and closed her eyes. "Perfect." She looked at Frances. "It's been so long since I had a cup of tea, you have no idea how much good that's doing me."

Frances was still sitting in the middle of the room. "Grandma, I-"

"I know, I know. You want to learn to read tea leaves-"

"No." Frances shook her head. "Zachary, my son, he has a school project on his family history." She unfolded a piece of paper. "I've some questions-"

"I can teach you love potions, and money drawing spells, and how to hex your enemies, and you want to know about the past?" Grandma set her cup back in the saucer with a clunk. "The past is dead and gone. It's the present you need to be worrying about —"

"He'd just like to know how you met Grandad."

Grandma set the tea on the arm of the chair and stood. "You want family history, go the library. Don't disturb my rest for such twaddle."

With a flicker of candles Grandma was gone.

Rag and Bone Man

"You there, Mr Tilley."

Charles was bent over the road, sifting through a rubbish pile for anything of value. He glanced up, straightening when he realised the man calling his name was Superintendent Normoyle.

"Mr Normoyle, sir."

"What've you got in the cart there?"

"Jus' some ol' bones, sir." Charles opened the chaff bag in his cart. "Ones I bought from some kids, others I picked along the roadside."

"You ain't taken any from Laidlaw's slaughter yards, have you?"

"No, sir."

Normoyle began picking through the bones and Charles' heart began to pound. He took a deep breath. Nothin' to be worried about.

"Which children did they come from?"

"The Harris kids. They've permission to gather from Mr Ford's farm, I believe."

"Mm-hm." Normoyle pulled a bone out of the bag. "This skull 'ere. Laidlaw's the only fellow about these parts who cuts the horns in such a way."

Charles' breath caught in his throat, and he coughed to clear it. "I don't know nothin' 'bout Mr Laidlaw's methods, sir. But I know where 'is fences are, and I ain't ever taken anything from 'is side of 'em."

Normoyle shook his head. "I'm sorry to do this to you Mr Tilley, but I'll have to take your cart and let Mr Laidlaw have a look. If it ain't his, all'll be well."

Charles shook his head. "I need the cart, sir. Can't carry enough meself. Don't make much outta it."

"I'll be in touch." Superintendent Normoyle tipped his hat as he took the handle of Charles' cart.

"I've a wife 'n two kids ta feed." Charles called, watching Superintendent Normoyle take his livelihood away up the street. "We just lost a little-un."

Normoyle glanced back. "Then you have one less mouth to feed, don't you?" He gave a sharp nod of his head and disappeared around the corner, leaving Charles to fight the growing pit of despair in his stomach.

Undoing Life's Choices

"Ready?"

Walter nodded. "Am I ever."

They approached the children playing in the yard.

"Daddy's home!" The excited squeals were well worth the gut-churning journey in the time-machine, the struggle to convince his younger self not to make those terrible choices.

It took Walter time to recognise the man embracing his children; the face unmarked by anger, himself, after a different life.

"I don't understand."

"You wanted your family to have the loving father and husband they deserve. You sent your life along a different course."

Walter's skin tingled, and he realised his body was fading.

"You no longer exist."

Whispered Goodbye

All signs of existence had been cleaned away. All memories altered. It was for the best, but still, Binah wished it could be different. She'd loved this family, so much more than any of the thousands of others she'd helped, and for the first time she wanted to be remembered. But there were more families who needed her aid; more scars to heal; lives to save. She sighed and turned away. Had she seen the youngest head lift at the sound she might have remained, but her eyes were downcast as she departed, with nothing more than a whispered goodbye.

Emergency

"Emergency."

"Yokai National Park, about an hour along the trail. There's a woman calling for help."

"Do not approach. We're on our way."

Hiroshi ignores the ridiculous instruction, and follows the voice to a cave entrance.

"Help."

He switches on his torch.

At the back of the cave, a pale face, tears reflecting the torchlight.

He reaches her, and she wraps her arms around him.

Something sharp pierces his neck. He pulls away, too late. Her arms are long black spindles, six more wrap him in strong silky thread.

"Foolish, tasty humans." She cackles, as his body looses all sensation.

Dancing in Time

'Dusk is when the magic happens, the time between times, neither night nor day. The between is always where the magic happens, neither here nor there. And the shore is the most magical of all, the meeting point of earth and sea and sky, and the shore at dusk is most potent for stepping through to some where, or some when, else.'

'Mm-hm.' Carmel tried not to frown. Jack was clearly interested in what he was telling her, even if he wasn't making a whole lot of sense. She'd loved that about him once, his enthusiasm and excitement for obscure topics, but there were a lot of decades between now and then. Maybe she was just getting old.

'Time travel never had to be invented. It's not a technology. It's a magic that needs to be discovered, and I have.'

'Right.' Her eyebrow twitched, and she fought to keep the skepticism from her face.

This was not the date she'd expected. A picnic on the beach at twilight was perfect, but this diatribe on liminal space and time travel was not her cup of tea. She remembered Jack as she'd once known him, all romance back then. The dances they'd attended when they were courting were still some of her happiest memories.

'I'm sorry.' he sighed. 'I'm boring you, aren't I?'

She tried to object but he held up his hand and she stopped.

'You used to love the dances back in the day. Do you remember? They were right here, on this beach.' He stood and held out his hand, pulling her to stand up. Moonlight reflected off the waves, and then the air shimmered and through the haze came lights and people and movement, and a moment later, melody. She gasped.

'Is that... us?' She pointed to a young couple jiving in the middle of the dance floor.

He grinned. 'It will only last for an evening... join me?'

Her eyes welled with tears as she nodded, and they stepped through together, just another older couple dancing in the corner.

The Cyclist

A shower of gravel sprays across the ditch, alerting the robin to the human presence. The thud sends her circling above, her attention drawn to the slowing tick of whirring spokes. Breeze ruffles uncovered hair. She alights on a post and peers at the human. Few exist these days, and she wants a closer look at this one, lying so still, but there's a glistening red over the gravel and a warning tang in the air. Robin knows the slowing pulse of it will call others, less curious and more hungry.

She won't hang around for that.

Well of Forgetting

Deep beneath the waves, out past the edge of the conti-
nental shelf, the dead queue, awaiting their time to pass
through the well of forgetting and be reborn.

Not all want to forget. Some fight for the chance to
carry their memories over. Sometimes, if they've proven
themselves in life, the god of the dead grants them their
memory.

Written for #mastoprompt: #underneath

First Published 20 November 2022

The Consequences of Climate Change on the Merpeople

The whole school of bright coloured fish darted out of reach.

They were deeper than they ought've been, harder to catch, sent into cooler waters by warming coastal currents.

Ineska had fed from the generosity of other merfolk until they threatened her with starvation if she didn't pull her own weight.

Colour stood out in the gloom, and Ineska launched her net. It caught, snagged.

Pulling it loose, her finger sliced along a sharp rock.

She'd never seen her own blood.

Her catch spilled free, a shadow loomed, and she remembered, too late, the danger in this patch of sea.

Dissect

The green-tinged skin parted with ease as the blade skimmed the surface.

The internal space was examined: an empty cavity where the back of the lungs and rib cage should have been, a soft fleshy slit at the sternum, a sac filled with what could have been honey.

The examiner stepped back and glanced at his companions.

'I've never seen anything like it.'

As they watched, the bits melded back together, skin zipping itself back up.

The creature sat.

'Perhaps it's time you humans admitted you don't know everything?'

They nodded, wide-eyed, as it stood up, and vanished.

The Cailleach

A single eye peered between strands of brittle grey hair covering the hag's brilliant blue face.

"You seek to visit the dead?"

Tally's heart raced. "Yes."

"You can't bring them back."

She took a deep breath and held the old woman's gaze. "I want to ask a question."

The eye narrowed. "Can you answer one?"

Tally swallowed. "I don't know."

"Who am I?"

"Y-you are the Cailleach," Tally stuttered. "Grandmother of all the gods."

The crone frowned. "What will you ask?"

"Why did she leave?" The child's voice broke.

The Cailleach's gaze softened, and she pulled Tally into a comforting embrace.

"It was time."

Blessed

A tawny frogmouth perches on the fallen tree. An echidna ambles past me, stopping to tap it's beak against my bare foot, whether to find out what I am, or say hello, I don't know. Wallabies eat the grass, so we don't have to mow. Frogs and fairy wrens sing their chorus. As I garden, the horses next door wander over to say hello. I bite into an apple, from a tree planted years ago by a previous inhabitant of this house, and I take a moment to acknowledge just how blessed I really am.

Thank you!

Thank you for reading my odd collection of tiny tales. If you enjoyed these, you might enjoy my other short stories – mostly published on Medium, but also in various other places around the internet and in anthologies.

More information about myself and my work can be found at my website: https://heatherewings.com.au. And if you'd like to be kept up-to-date on my latest stories, visit the link below to sign up to my newsletter for my most up to date news.

https://mailchi.mp/239101cbfce3/3m28dn9jhp

Acknowledgements

Each of these stories has been previously published, in the following places:

Not Entirely Human – Microcosm, 28 January 2022 (Written for the Microcosm Prompt 'Lyin' about the Dyin')

One Wish – Microcosm, 16 August 2022 (Written for the #Auswrites prompt: a tweet length story featuring the words 'watermelon' and 'anxiety'.)

Shadows – Medium, 19 November 2022

Rescue – Japanese Fantasy Drabbles, Insignia Stories, April 2020

Who Caught Who – Japanese Fantasy Drabbles, Insignia Stories, April 2020

Christmas Wedding – Medium, 20 July 2021 (Written for a Family History Flash Fiction assignment, 2015)

Weaving Fate – Microcosm, 2 Aug 2022 (Written for Microcosm's prompt: The Story Spider)

Arthur Gordon – Medium, 25 July 2021 (Written for a Family History Flash Fiction assignment, 2015)

Tea with Grandma – Lite Lit One, 14 December 2018 (This story has a sequel of sorts... 'Whiskey for Great Grandma'. If you're interested, you can find it on Medium)

Rag and Bone Man – Medium, 25 November 2022 (Written for a Family History Flash Fiction assignment, 2015)

Undoing Life's Choices – 'Chronos: An Anthology of Time Drabbles', Shacklebound Books, 1 September 2018 (This story inspired my novella 'Fixing Kendra', which received an Honourable Mention in the Stillhouse Press 2022 Novella Competition)

Whispered Goodbye – Microcosm, 21 November 2022

Emergency – 'Japanese Fantasy Drabbles', Insignia Stories, April 2020

Dancing in Time – The Power of Poetry, 23 November 2022 (Written for #mastoprompt: #liminal)

The Cyclist – Medium, 18 November 2022 (Written for the Digital Writers Festival Microfiction Competition 2018)

Well of Forgetting – Medium, 20 November 2022 (Written for #mastoprompt: #underneath)

The Consequences of Climate Change on the Merpeople – Oceans: Dark Drabbles #9, Black Hare Press, 14 April 2020

Dissect – Microcosm, 16 November 2022 (Written for #mastoprompt: #dissect)

Cailleach – Medium, 28 November 2022

Blessed – Medium, 27 November 2022

About the Author

Heather Ewings is an Australian author of speculative fiction, with a MA in History and a fascination with myth and folklore. Her short stories have been published widely, including Microcosm, Lit Lite One, and Deadset Press. Her debut novella 'What the Tide Brings' was printed as part of The People's Library in 2018, and later published in 2020. In 2022 she received an Honorable Mention in the Stillhouse Press Novella Competition, for her story 'Fixing Kendra'. Heather lives among gum trees and wattles, where she balances her time between writing, home schooling her youngest child, making beeswax candles, and attempting to grow a bit of food.